In the year 776 BC, the first
Olympic Games were held in a town
called Olympia in Ancient Greece.
Many years later, a boy named Olly
grew up there, dreaming of being
an Olympic champion. But first,
he would have to be better than his
arch-enemy, Spiro...

ORCHARD BOOKS
338 Euston Road, London NW1 3BH
Orchard Books Australia
Level 17/207 Kent Street, Sydney, NSW 2000

First published in 2011
First paperback publication in 2012

ISBN 978 1 40831 181 3 (hardback)
ISBN 978 1 40831 189 9 (paperback)

Text and illustrations © Shoo Rayner 2011

The right of Shoo Rayner to be identified as the author and
illustrator of this work has been asserted by him in accordance
with the Copyright, Designs and Patents Act, 1988.

A CIP catalogue record for this book is available
from the British Library.

1 3 5 7 9 10 8 6 4 2 (hardback)
1 3 5 7 9 10 8 6 4 2 (paperback)

Printed in Great Britain

Orchard Books is a division of Hachette Children's Books,
an Hachette UK company.
www.hachette.co.uk

OLYMPIA

JUMP FOR GLORY

SHOO RAYNER

ORCHARD

CHAPTER ONE

"It's so hot and I'm so tired," said Olly, slumping under a tree. "I can't lift anything any more!"

"You're a wimp," his arch-enemy, Spiro, taunted. He picked up a couple of weights and held them above his head. "You're just a useless *little worm*."

Olly ignored Spiro. He wasn't worth arguing with. Olly sat back in the shade and watched as Makedon, the greatest jumper of them all, made his final long jump of the day at the athletes' training ground.

Makedon powered down the runway, pumping the heavy stones he carried as if they were feathers. He hit the board, took off and sailed through the air.

The tall, gangly athlete swung his arms backwards and threw the heavy stones behind him. He seemed to float like a leaf, then crashed into the sandpit below. He stood up, looked at where he had landed and punched the air.

"I'm still the best!" Makedon proclaimed. "The spirits are with me!"

"Wow!" Olly muttered under his breath. "That was amazing."

"OK, lads," Ariston called to Olly and Spiro. "It's the Boys' Jumping Competition next week. You've got ten minutes for a bit more practice before lunchtime."

Ariston was Olly's dad. He ran the gymnasium in Olympia, the town where the Olympic Games were held every four years.

Olly and Spiro worked at the gym, doing all sorts of odd jobs. They also learned skills from some of the world's greatest athletes who trained there.

Olly only had one ambition in life. One day, he wanted to be an Olympic champion.

But today he was exhausted. It was too hot and he could barely pick up his lightweight jumping stones.

"Come on, Olly!" his dad called. "Let's see you do your best."

Olly placed his thumbs in the carved grooves on his stones and gripped them as tightly as he could.

He counted thirty paces, added a little bit extra for luck, and turned to face the sandpit.

Sweat beaded on Olly's forehead as he started down the runway. His arms dangled uselessly by his side. He had no strength left to swing the stones in time with his run-up. One of the stones slipped from his grasp and Olly stumbled and tripped.

Spiro laughed. "Ha! You'll never be a jumper, weakling!"

Spiro picked up his stones and swung them around with ease. He counted out his paces, roared down the runway and made a perfect jump. "I'll always beat you, skinny muscles!" he teased Olly.

"Dad!" Olly said. "I've been lifting the stones all morning and my arms feel like they're made of stone too! Do I have to use the jumping stones?"

Ariston stroked his beard and thought for a moment. "Well...I don't suppose you do. The stones help you go further when you throw them behind you mid-jump. But it's not a rule or anything. Go on then, one last try without them."

It was still hot and Olly was still exhausted, but at least he didn't have to carry those stones! He focussed on the sandpit and started his run.

"Weakling!" Spiro yelled.

That does it! Olly thought. "I'll show you!" he growled, as he pumped his arms and zoomed down the runway. He hit the board and pushed himself into the air. He kicked his legs and flailed his arms to try and leap that little bit further.

"Well done!" called Ariston. "That was almost as good as Spiro!"

"Huh!" Spiro muttered, as he collected up the stones and put them in a wheelbarrow. "He'll never be as good as me."

"Can you use anything to help you jump?" Olly asked his dad, as they carried the heavy jumping stones back to the changing rooms.

"I don't see why not," Ariston replied. "There's really only one rule: you have to jump from the board and go as far as you can."

"There's nothing you can do to beat me," Spiro sneered as he parked the wheelbarrow behind the changing rooms.

"I'll beat you one day!" Olly said defiantly. "And that's a promise!"

"OK, lads. That's enough," said Ariston. "It's time you were laying the tables for the athletes' lunch."

CHAPTER TWO

As Olly laid the tables, he couldn't help eating a few pine nuts from one of the salad bowls. Pine nuts were his favourite.

Just then, Makedon came in. He saw Olly and laughed. "Hoping our food will make you a great athlete like us, are you?" he said.

Makedon's friends laughed, too. Olly felt his cheeks glow red with embarrassment. All Olly wanted was to be a champion like Makedon.

As the athletes ate their food, Simonedes, their old and wrinkled history teacher, told them stories about heroes and gods and all the things they got up to. Olly loved this part of the day. He could listen to Simonedes' stories forever.

"Do you remember Theseus?"
Simonedes began.

The athletes raised their cups
and shouted, "Yes! We remember
Theseus!"

Of course they remember Theseus,
thought Olly. They had heard tales
about him since they were in their
cradles. Theseus was the hero who
killed the Minotaur in the maze.
He found his way back out of the
maze by winding up a ball of wool
given to him by Princess Ariadne.

Simonedes smiled and continued. "Theseus had many adventures in his life. In Theseus's time, there was a man called Sinis the Pine Bender who lived near Corinth, on the narrow strip of land that separates the two halves of Greece.

"Sinis was a bad man. He would ask passing travellers to help him bend down pine trees. When they weren't expecting it, Sinis would let go. The trees sprang back and the poor travellers were hurled into the air. They would be crushed upon the rocks or drowned in the sea below."

"Urrgh!" the athletes cheered. They'd heard this story before, but they loved it!

Olly knew the story, too. He looked up at the paintings that decorated the walls of the dining room. There was Sinis, a giant of a man, bending down a pine tree, and a surprised-looking traveller hurtling through the air!

Simonedes smiled and carried on. "But it was Sinis's unlucky day when he asked Theseus to help him. Theseus turned the tables on Sinis. He pulled the pine trees down to the ground and tied Sinis's arms and legs to them. Sinis was strong, but he grew tired.

"When Sinis could no longer hold the pine trees, they snapped back and ripped that bad, bad man into pieces, much to the joy of the vultures, who lived close by and feasted on his body!"

"Hooray!" the athletes cheered.

"Thanks to Theseus," Simonedes continued, "the path is now safe and travellers can reach their journey's end in one piece."

Olly looked up at another painting of Theseus. He was so strong and handsome. Olly imagined looking like him when he was grown up and wearing the olive leaf crown of an Olympic champion.

"Watch out, weakling," Spiro sneered, as he barged past Olly with a pile of dirty plates. Olly stumbled and dropped a half-empty salad bowl on the floor.

"I'm still going to beat you!" Olly yelled defiantly.

The athletes had finished eating and were filing out of the room. "Are you strong enough to pick up lettuce leaves today, Olly?" Makedon joked. His friends roared with laughter.

Olly felt like a worm. Fuming, he picked up the mess and finished clearing the tables. It was the last job of the day. Then the afternoon was all his own.

CHAPTER THREE

Olly's sister, Chloe, found him in the
courtyard outside the gym.

"Oh, Olly! What's the matter now?"
Chloe sighed.

Olly scowled and kicked the sandy
ground. "I hate Spiro," he growled.
"And Makedon. He was
making fun of me and
all the athletes were
laughing. I can't help
it if I'm not as strong
as Spiro – he's a year
older than me and
he's built like a stupid,
thick-headed ox!"

Chloe rolled her eyes. She'd put up with Olly and Spiro's battle to be the best for years.

"It's too hot to be angry," she soothed. "Why don't we go up to the forest? It's cooler there and we can swim in the lake. If you stay out in the sun, your head is going to cook!"

Olly shrugged his shoulders and said nothing, but he followed his sister along the path that led to the shady woods.

Insects chirruped in the trees and butterflies flew around their heads as they climbed up to the cooler air.

"You're a much better athlete than Spiro," Chloe said. She was used to boosting Olly's confidence after his fights with Spiro.

"But he always beats me!" Olly said.

"That's because he's bigger and stronger than you – but he doesn't have your ability – and he doesn't have your brains! You'll beat him one day, with practice, skill and the right spirit."

"Hmpf!" Olly grunted. Deep down he knew Chloe was right, but it felt like it would be a lifetime before he was ever strong enough to beat Spiro at jumping.

"I wish I could enter the competition," said Chloe, leaping across boulders like a gazelle. "If you think it's unfair that you always have to compete against Spiro, how unfair is it that I'm not allowed to jump at all?"

"Ha!" Olly snorted. "That's because you're a girl – girls can't do sport in Olympia!"

"Well, they should be allowed to!" Chloe said angrily. She launched herself off a rock and sailed gracefully through the air.

Olly had to admit that she had a really good jumping style.

Thunk!

Olly and Chloe stopped in their tracks.

"What was that?" Chloe hissed.

Thunk!

"It sounds like an axe," Olly whispered.

The children crept through the
undergrowth, following the sound.

"There!" Chloe pointed.

In the clearing beside the lake,
a huge man was swinging an axe,
hacking large chunks out of a tree.

"He's enormous!" Chloe whispered.

"He looks like Sinis the Pine Bender!" Olly croaked, thinking of the painting in the dining hall.

Thunk! The axe bit deep into the tree trunk. The tree creaked and groaned, and slowly began to sway and move. Then it picked up speed and, with a roaring rush, it crashed to the ground.

Silence filled the space where the tree had stood. The birds stopped singing. Olly and Chloe held their breath.

Suddenly, the dead branch that Olly was standing on snapped with a loud *CRACK!*

"Who's there?" the man boomed. "Come out now! I can see you!" He swung the axe menacingly round his head. The sun glinted on the razor-sharp blade.

Olly knew he should run, but he felt almost hypnotised by the man's demand. He and Chloe slipped out of their hiding place and staggered into the sunshine.

"Spying on me, were you?" the giant growled.

"N-n-no, sir!" Olly stammered.

"W-w-we w-were coming to have a swim in the lake!" Chloe shook with fear.

The man stared at them suspiciously. His enormous, black eyebrows furrowed on his forehead.

"Y-y-you're not Sinis the Pine Bender, are you?" Olly asked bravely.

The man's eyebrows shot up in surprise. He stared at Olly and Chloe. Then, as if he'd only just realised they were children, he burst out laughing.

"No! I'm Leon, the tree cutter,"
he told them. "I get a bit spooked
working on my own in the forest. You
never know when someone might
jump out of the bushes and…" His
voice trailed off. He looked all around
to check no one was listening. "There
are spirits living in the trees, you
know," he whispered.

Leon was enormous. Olly couldn't
imagine him being scared of anything.

"I bet you can bend pine trees,
though," Chloe said, looking at Leon's
powerful muscles.

Leon found a thin pine tree that was growing near the water's edge. He reached up and began to pull the top of the tree towards the ground. "I can bend little trees like this!" he laughed.

Chloe clapped her hands. "Hold it right there," she said. "I've got an idea!"

CHAPTER FOUR

Leon pulled the top of the tree almost down to the ground.

Chloe ran over and sat on it. "Let go!" she ordered.

"But…" Leon looked worried.

"That looks dangerous, Chloe," Olly warned. "You'll hurt yourself, and you are only a—"

"What? Only a GIRL?" Chloe's eyes flashed angrily.

Olly could tell that Chloe wasn't going to listen to him. She was very determined.

"I'll be fine," Chloe frowned. "Now. Let go-o-o-o-o-o!"

As Leon let go, the pine tree arced up to its full height, hurling Chloe into the air.

At the top of the curve, Chloe let go. With grace and beauty, she sailed through the air like an eagle, before landing in the middle of the lake with a loud scream and an almighty splash.

"*Wahoooooh!*"

Olly and Leon watched in horror as the water closed over Chloe's head.

Olly was about to make Leon dive in and save his sister from drowning, when her head broke the surface and she let out a squeal of joy.

"That was a-ma-zing!" she yelled. "Let's do again!"

It looked so much fun. Olly was desperate to have a go himself. He looked up at Leon.

"Can I do it? Please? Pretty please?" he begged.

Leon rolled his eyes and accepted his fate. Today, he was Leon the Pine Bender!

Sailing through the air, Olly imagined he was jumping for glory, a champion of the Olympic Games!

The hot, sticky afternoon
disappeared in an endless round
of pine-tree diving.

"Again! Again! Again!" Chloe said,
laughing.

"I'm getting tired," Leon
complained, reaching his huge arms
up into the tree and pulling it down to
the ground again. "This is definitely
the last time."

The tree groaned…and moaned…
and creaked…and groaned again
until suddenly…*CRACK!*

The thin tree trunk could take no
more of the strain. It snapped and fell
to the ground. The afternoon's fun
was over.

The hot sunshine soon had Olly and Chloe dry again. Sitting on the warm rocks, they watched Leon pick up his axe and trim the branches off the tree trunk.

"Can I have that piece there?" Olly asked, pointing at a straight length from the top of the tree.

Leon picked it up and passed it to Olly. "It's not much use to me," he said. "Not thick enough for firewood."

The pole was was about twice Olly's height. Olly tested it and felt its springiness.

"The spirit of the tree is still alive in this. I can feel it," Olly smiled.

Holding the thinnest end of the pole in both hands, Olly charged at the lake. As he reached the water's edge, he stuck the end of the pole into the ground and jumped.

The pole bent under his weight, then sprang back into shape, hurling him high into the air and – *splash!* – into the water again.

"You're the Pine Bender now, are you?" Leon laughed.

Olly and Chloe spent the rest of the day flying through the air, splashing into the lake. By the time the sun began to set, their arms ached like never before, but they were happy.

"You'd best go home before it gets dark," Leon advised.

"Will you come and watch me at the Boys' Jumping Competition?" Olly asked. "I'll take my jumping pole with me!"

"We'll see," chuckled Leon.

CHAPTER FIVE

A week later, before the jumping competition got underway, Olly was talking to the the judges.

"So, if I don't have to use jumping stones," Olly reasoned, "it must be all right for me to use a stick instead."

The judges stroked their beards and thought about it, but they couldn't deny the logic of Olly's argument. There wasn't much difference between sticks and stones.

Olly took his place at the end of the runway for his first jump. Each boy had three attempts. Whoever jumped the furthest would win.

Olly began his run-up. As his foot hit the board, he stuck his pole into the ground and lifted off.

The pole bent, then sprang back into shape. Olly felt the spirit of the tree catapult him twice as far as the all-time boys' jumping record!

"That's cheating!" Spiro snarled. He grabbed the pole from Olly. "Here, let me try."

Spiro stormed down the runway, holding Olly's pole in front of him. He dug the pole into the ground and put all of his weight on it. But Spiro was heavier than Olly. The pole bent – and kept on bending. Spiro was suspended in midair, waiting for the pole to spring back again.

Instead, with a slow cracking sound, the pole snapped in two. Spiro collapsed on the sand with a heavy thud.

The judges went into a huddle and had a long discussion.

"We applaud Olly's new style of jumping," Ariston announced. "But we feel it does not suit the Boys' Jumping Competition."

Olly's heart sank.

"We will start the competition again with new rules," said Ariston. "This time there will be no weights or any other means of assistance. The jumper must rely purely on their skill and strength."

"And spirit!" Olly muttered under his breath.

The new competition got underway. After the other boys had done their three jumps, Spiro was firmly in the lead. Olly could see Spiro's marker on the edge of the sandpit. His own was just a short distance behind it.

Olly screwed his eyes up in concentration for his last and final jump. "I can do it!" he told himself.

CHAPTER SIX

Olly touched the two halves of the jumping pole and felt the spirit of the tree surge through his muscles.

Imagining that he was carrying the pole with him, Olly stormed down the runway for the last time. "I am Olly the Pine Bender!" he roared inside his head.

Olly imagined stabbing the pole into the ground as he leaped off the jumping board. He felt the spirit of the pine tree pushing him higher and further than he had ever jumped before.

Olly crashed into the sandpit and rolled forward. Turning to see how far he had gone, Olly caught the look on Spiro's face. Spiro was red with rage. Olly knew he had beaten him!

The judges announced that Olly was the winner. Olly punched the air and the crowd cheered as his father placed the olive leaf crown on his head.

Chloe rushed up and hugged him. "That was incredible!" she cheered.

Leon emerged from the crowd and swept Olly up onto his shoulders. He ran round the stadium with him in a lap of honour.

"Well done, Olly!" Leon laughed. "You are the Pine Bender. And may the spirit of the pine tree stay with you forever!"

OLYMPIC FACTS!

DID YOU KNOW...?

The ancient Olympic Games began over 2,700 years ago in Olympia, in southwest Greece.

The ancient Games were were held in honour of Zeus, king of the gods, and were staged every four years at Olympia.

The long jump was originally good training for war. Warriors needed to leap over streams and ravines when they were on the attack!

Long jump athletes used carved stones called *halteres* to help them create momentum to fly through the air.

The ancient Olympics inspired the modern Olympic Games, which began in 1896 in Athens, Greece. Today, the modern Olympic Games are still held every four years in a different city around the world.

SHOO RAYNER

RUN LIKE THE WIND	978 1 40831 179 0
WRESTLE TO VICTORY	978 1 40831 180 6
JUMP FOR GLORY	978 1 40831 181 3
THROW FOR GOLD	978 1 40831 182 0
SWIM FOR YOUR LIFE	978 1 40831 183 7
RACE FOR THE STARS	978 1 40831 184 4
ON THE BALL	978 1 40831 185 1
DEADLY TARGET	978 1 40831 186 8

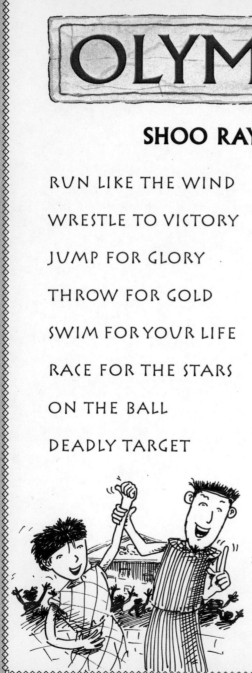

All priced at £8.99

Orchard Books are available
from all good bookshops, or can
be ordered from our website,
www.orchardbooks.co.uk,
or telephone 01235 827702,
or fax 01235 827703.